DISCOVER THE DEMON DIARIES,
WHICH HAS SPELLBOUND 2.5 MILLION READERS.

A HINT of

HELL

BEWITCHED BY CHRISTMAS

A CHRISTMAS STORY IN
THE DEMON DIARIES

CLAIRE CHILTON

Bibliography
Dickens, Charles. (2006).
A Christmas Carol.
Urbana, Illinois: Project Gutenberg.
Retrieved June 21, 2019, from:
http://www.gutenberg.org/files/19337/19337-h/19337-h.htm.

MORE BOOKS

THE DEMON DIARIES
A Hint of Magic
Bewitched by Magic

Demonic Dora
Bewitched in Hell

Deceased Dora
Bewitched in Death

Divine Dora
Bewitched in Heaven

A Hint of Hell
Bewitched by Christmas

"Every idiot who goes about with 'Merry Christmas' on his lips, should be boiled with his own pudding, and buried with a stake of holly through his heart."

−*A Christmas Carol*
Charles Dickens (2006) p15

1

BLOODY LATE AGAIN

K ieron Lascher hurried through the streets of Hell, bustling past a range of colorful demons with his heart hammering and a cold sweat forming on his brow.

Please let me make it. I can't be late. If I fail this exam, I'm screwed!

His pulse was racing as he dashed past the array of stores, his black robes flapping behind him.

He skidded around the corner of the Zombie Emporium, his eyes meeting with those of a talking head in the window as he turned onto Fifth Street. The head's mouth opened and closed, baring rotting yellow teeth as it continued to speak soundlessly through the glass.

He shook his head and stared down the road.

His heart stopped beating for a moment when he saw the flames bursting out of the rocket-like exhaust pipes on the back of the school bus.

No, no, no!

He lunged down the road as the fiery rockets flared up when the bus pulled away from the curb.

He jumped into the gutter to avoid the crowds milling on the sidewalk, running at full speed to reach the bus before it left him behind. He pumped his arms, using every ounce of energy he had.

Not today, I can't be late today!

His heart pounded as he neared the black and red vehicle, the words on the bumper sticker becoming clearer.

'Move or die, bitches!'

He was gaining on the vehicle, but he knew it wouldn't be for long.

Come on. You can make it.

A few feet from the back of it, he leapt into the air, reaching out for the barbed black grill on the back.

A loud squeal to his left caused him to turn his

2

head at the last moment.

Gore, blood and bits of bone splatted him with a force that sent him flying sideways and knocked him onto the sidewalk.

Blinded by red goop, he wiped the mulch out of his eyes and stared in horror as the bus drove away without him.

I'm a dead demon.

He stared down at his sodden robes. They were drenched in blood and demon guts with bits of brown fur and flesh hanging off them.

He plucked a clump of fur off his robe and swallowed as he stared at it.

A familiar giggle echoed behind him.

He narrowed his eyes and glanced over his shoulder at the impish green demon, which was rolling around on the floor laughing.

"You again!"

It giggled and nodded. There were tears of laughter in its red glowing eyes.

"Seriously, every morning? You do this every fucking morning. Is this going to keep on happening?"

It rolled over and smiled at him, then eagerly nodded.

"There aren't any other demon lords that that you prefer to fuck with?"

Its grin widened as it shook its head.

Kieron sighed and offered it the clump of brown fur. "You want your friend back?"

It burst out laughing.

He dropped the fur onto the sidewalk and pushed himself off the ground.

Great, even hell spawn is better at evil than I am.

He knew exactly what had happened. It happened every morning. Whether he was waiting for the bus or late like today, the green demon would push its brown furry friend off the sidewalk and into oncoming traffic for the express purpose of splatting him all over Kieron.

"I don't know why Trevor is still friends with you," he muttered to the laughing demon as he plucked bits of Trevor off his robe and gently placed them in a pile on the sidewalk.

The demon guts began to meld together as Trevor reformed into a brown fluffy blob.

The green demon howled with laughter.

Disgusted by it all, Kieron turned and began walking down the street. Today wasn't the day for worrying over some blood spatter. It was mock exams this week. If he missed his exams in pure evil, his teacher and parents were going to roast him alive.

The Daemon Academia was too far away for him to make it in time. There was only one option.

He closed his eyes and exhaled.

I can't believe I'm going to do this.

He headed down the street towards the glowing red storefront ahead. Flames shot out onto the sidewalk in front of the store. Parked at the curb, were a line of motorcycles with hellish pictures emblazoned across them.

He stopped beside the nearest bike with a sigh.

There was a slog beast seated on the vehicle. Its piggish face was covered in dark fur, and its black beard trailed from its chin in a long plait.

"Ready to ride, little …" He trailed off as he stared at Kieron.

"I need to buy a ride," Kieron muttered.

"Eww, no, look at the state of you." The slog

beast shook its furry head.

"Come on, man. I can pay."

The creature narrowed its big brown eyes. "You'll actually pay for yourself to ride?"

"Sure." Kieron nodded. Most demons only paid to punish someone else on a hog ride, but he was desperate.

The slog beast eyed him. "Alright, but if your head breaks off, I don't give refunds."

Kieron gave a nod of understanding before he climbed onto the back of the motorbike. "Just get me to the Daemon Academia before nine. I don't care if my head is attached as long as I get there."

The slog beast's large fangs glistened as he broadly smiled. "I can do fast."

Kieron clung to the slog beast as they shot through a tunnel of fire at break-neck speed. His body jolted off the motorbike when the driver plowed through a dimensional wall.

He tightened his grip on the piggish driver's waist, grasping at its worn leather jacket as his legs flew out behind him. Bursts of fire shot dangerously close to him, scorching his skin as the vehicle roared through the tunnel.

"Do you have to go so faaaaahhhh," he cried as the road of fire dropped out from beneath them, and they plummeted over the edge of a cliff into a deep black abyss before dropping down towards a field of thorns.

"We need to go fast, or you can't make the jump." The driver shouted back over his shoulder. "Plus, it's fun!"

Kieron whimpered as the motorcycle hit the ground, jolting his body and slamming his hips back onto the passenger seat.

Sharp thorns shredded his robes and skin as they plowed through the bushes towards the Highway to Hell.

Sweat beaded his brow and dribbled down into his eyes, but he didn't dare let go of the driver to wipe it away. The salty water stung his eyes, making him blink at the dark shape ahead.

Once his eyes had cleared, they widened in horror. "Truck! Truck!" He pointed to the oncoming monster truck that was zooming down the road ahead of them. They were heading straight towards a collision with the side of the truck.

The driver shook his head. "We'll make it."

"We'll make what?" Kieron asked incredulously as he clung to the bike with his thighs while it roared towards the side of the highway.

"The crossing." The driver shrugged.

"What crossing?" Kieron's heart hammered as their high-speed crash into the large black truck seemed imminent.

As the motorbike crossed the highway, he glanced sideways at bright headlights that were close enough to touch. The big rig roared its horn, and then it was gone as they slipped through another portal onto a quiet street in the magic district.

The driver pulled up to the curb and turned to face Kieron. "Delivered safe and sound." He smiled a toothy grin.

Kieron froze, the reflection of oncoming headlights still blinding his eyes.

Did we make it?

He blinked several times before noticing where he

was. Then he rolled off the back of the bike and fell to the ground. His stomach turned over, and he retched for a moment before forcing himself to stand.

"What? No thank you?" the driver said.

Kieron glanced down at the burning embers still glowing on his tattered robes. He brushed back his short blond hair, finding demon guts and soot caked into it. He turned to face the slog beast.

"Thank you," he muttered, dropping three dark-soul-chips into the driver's hand before turning and staggering up the steps of the academy.

He heard the slog beast laugh as he staggered sideways like a crab when his legs refused to work properly.

He glanced up at the large clock on the front of the majestic building.

At least I made it here in time.

He gripped the railing, pulling himself up the stone stairs towards his classroom.

Just a few more steps.

"Where the hell do you think you're going looking like that?" A cold voice startled him.

He glanced up to see the dark robes of a professor.

9

His heart plummeted into his stomach as he realized it was Professor Kazaik.

Great, the one person who would rather gut me than help me with this exam.

"Er, to my mock exams," Kieron muttered.

Kazaik scowled at him with a deadly glint in his dark eyes. "If you try to enter my classroom in that state, I will eviscerate you."

PURE EVIL

K ieron was certain he was having a panic
attack as he stared at the clock on the wall.
His throat had closed up, and a cold sweat
covered his body.

How has it been forty minutes already?

He could have sworn that he'd only just sat down
at his desk. After Kazaik had made him use a cleansing
spell to remove the soot and blood from himself and
his robe, he'd felt drained, but he was sure he hadn't
passed out.

Is there a time spell on this room?

He rubbed his palms against his now clean robe to
remove the cold sweat from them while glancing
around the classroom. Several of the students were

hunched over their papers, each scribbling down answers with frowns on their faces.

He noticed Carlisle Smythe reclining back in his seat with a wide grin on his face. His exam was turned over, clearly finished.

Kieron narrowed his eyes at the red-faced demon lord. Carlisle got all the luck. He aced every test, and his horns had grown in early. Although he wasn't showing them today, he already looked like an adult demon when he went into demon form.

His father swore that the boy had matured faster because of his knack for evil.

Kieron shook his head. Carlisle was a mean asshole. There was a big difference between the beauty of pure magic and being snarky. The one thing that Kieron was good at was magic. There wasn't a spell in existence that he didn't know. He could do things with magic that no other demon could compete with. So what if he wasn't trying to take over Hell and hurt others. Surely, the point of being a good demon was being able to control magic.

Unfortunately, no one else in Hell seemed to appreciate how much he studied or what he had learned. They just saw the beauty in brutality.

Carlisle must have noticed him watching because he pointed to Kieron, and then drew a line across his throat with a meaty fist, indicating that Kieron was a dead man.

Kieron narrowed his eyes at the over-sized demon lord.

Carlisle smiled, and his fangs popped over his top lip as his eyes glowed red.

Kieron rolled his eyes and glanced down at the paper

Horn size isn't everything, dickwad.

He picked up his pencil.

I'll show them all.

He gritted his teeth. He'd studied hard, and he knew the spells. This should be easy. He stared at the paper.

NAME:

Okay, I know that.

He began to write his name on the dotted line, but the pencil broke on the 'L' in Lascher. He scanned his desk for a pencil sharpener, widening his eyes when he couldn't see one.

He heard Carlisle chuckle. He glanced back and saw the demon twirling his pencil sharpener in his hand.

Come on! Are you kidding me?

He glanced up at the clock. Ten minutes had passed by, and he hadn't even got his name right yet.

No, no, no!

He narrowed his eyes. There was definitely something hinky about that clock.

He peered up towards the front of the classroom. Professor Kazaik was standing behind his desk, scanning the room with hawk-like eyes. His black hair snaked down his back in swirling tendrils, and there was an evil gleam in his dark eyes.

Kieron considered asking the professor for a pencil sharpener, but shook his head at the thought. Kazaik had set a student on fire for asking to go to the bathroom in one of his classes before. Asking him for a pencil sharpener would only lead to a slow and painful death.

Kieron didn't have time resurrect himself before

the exams were over. Plus, a slow and painful death sucked ass.

Time to demon-up, son. His father's voice echoed in his mind. *And stop being so fucking wet.*

He scowled at his desk. His father would say that. He thought being nice was a flaw. He was appalled that he'd fathered demon spawn that excelled in reading magic books.

Kieron inhaled and glanced down at the broken pencil. Magic was the only answer though. "Whittle," he whispered under his breath, and the pencil spun in his hand as it sharpened itself on fresh air.

He smiled.

I can do this.

He frowned when the pencil continued to sharpen as the whittle spell ate it up in his hand, turning it into a nub.

"Shit, stop er, Haltus," he hissed.

The pencil stopped turning, leaving him an inch of pencil to work with.

He glanced up and noticed that Kazaik had narrowed his eyes, and they were focused on him.

The use of magic was banned during exams. The professor's eyes began to glow red.

"Concealous," Kieron muttered, covering the essence of his magic with a veil.

The professor scowled for a few more seconds before turning to scan the room again.

Kieron exhaled. Then he clenched the tiny pencil remains between his thumb and forefinger, scowling at it. Ignoring the clock and the fear that was bubbling up in his stomach, he quickly scrawled the rest of his name on the front of the exam paper and flipped it open.

Okay, question one.

He scanned the page. At the top, the title read:

PURE EVIL
LEVEL ONE MOCK EXAMINATION

He exhaled slowly in an attempt to combat his rattled nerves before reading the first question on the sheet.

WHEN FACED WITH A DYING ADVERSARY, DO

YOU:

A) FINISH HIM OFF WITH A DEATH CURSE.
B) MAKE HIM SUFFER IN A GRUESOME MANNER BEFORE FINALLY KILLING HIM.
C) HEAL HIS WOUNDS WITH A REVIVAL SPELL.
D) TAKE HIM OUT. AND THEN DESTROY HIS ENTIRE FAMILY AND ANY FUTURE GENERATIONS. CURSING THEM ALL WITH ETERNAL TORMENT.

Kieron pondered the question. Surely, it depended on the situation. If the adversary was going to come after him if he survived, then you'd have to finish him off to defend yourself, wouldn't you? But then, that might be acting too rashly. Better to heal him, and then see what happened. Maybe after you saved him, you'd become friends instead.

Shaking his head at how easy it was, he quickly circled 'C' and moved on to the next question. If they were all this easy, he'd ace this test in no time.

He glanced up at the clock, only five minutes remained until the exam would be over. Gritting his teeth, he focused on the exam and quickly rushed through all the questions with a smile on his face.

I can do this. The answers are obvious.

17

Kieron smiled at Kazaik as he handed his paper to him across the dark altar that the professor used for a desk. He was almost certain he'd aced the test, regardless of the obstacles in his way.

Kaziak's dark eyes settled on him in the form of a scowl. His long dark hair hung around his pale face in sharp strands. He snatched the paper out of Kieron's hand before glancing at the answers.

A cold shiver shot up Kieron's spine when a smile appeared on the professor's face.

That can't be a good thing.

The professor hated Kieron. He'd like nothing more than to see him fail.

"Er, everything okay?" Kieron asked.

"You'll get ten points for getting your name right." Kazaik closed his paper and glanced up at him with red glow in his eyes and a bright smile on his face.

He's just messing with me. Kieron told himself, but uncertainty crept into his mind. Maybe saving an adversary hadn't been the right answer, but surely, that's what any good demon would do?

He tried to ignore it, but worry knotted in his stomach. This was his last chance. If he failed another test, he wasn't going to escape punishment this time.

There were fifty questions. I can't have got them all wrong. I'll be fine.

He smiled at the professor and turned to leave the classroom.

"See you on Monday, sir." He called out behind him.

"I wouldn't count on it." He heard the professor mutter darkly behind him.

Kieron gulped down the panic bubbling in is throat.

What the hell does that mean?

HELLISH RESULTS

Kieron yelped and jumped back as the contents of his bathroom cabinet exploded out of it and onto the floor. He didn't jump back far enough. Several light boxes bounced off the top of his head before tumbling onto the floor.

He frowned and rubbed his head before kneeling down and plucking one of the boxes off the white tiles.

What the hell is all this crap?

He stared at the little black box, and his eyes widened in horror. The word 'Stud' was emblazoned across the front of box in garish yellow.

"What the fu—" He started to mutter, but was cut short by the sound of a terrifying scream echoing downstairs in Castle Lascher.

He narrowed his eyes and stood up.

My goddamn mother!

He opened the box and peered inside. It was filled with little foil packages, which he suspected were condoms. He rubbed his eyes and dropped the box onto the bathroom counter beside the sink.

I can't believe she filled my bathroom cabinets with fucking condoms.

He was painfully aware that his mother wanted to see him grow up to be a sexually deviant demon, but this was going too far. Was it too much to ask for a nice girl? Sure, he was fifteen and getting older every day, but he didn't want to date a trollop.

He shook his head. It was all about keeping up appearances for his mother. She wanted to brag at her next bridge game about how many girls Kieron had slept with.

He stared at his reflection in the mirror. His blue eyes were still widened in shock.

Fucking condoms!

He shook his head and knelt down to scoop up the fallen boxes before shoving them all back into the bathroom cabinet and slamming the door shut.

He'd been worrying about his exam results all week, and this was the last thing he needed. He already felt pressured to be something he wasn't, but now he was expected to date a skank just to keep his mother happy.

It wasn't that he didn't like girls. He liked them a bit too much by Hell standards. He wanted to be in love and meet a nice one. Was that an unreasonable thing to want?

He sighed again. It was in Hell. Love didn't exist here.

He idly wondered if other dimensions were better. He'd been born in Hell and had never been anywhere else, but there had to be somewhere better than this.

A deathly scream echoed through the castle again, causing him to jump. It sounded as if his mother was on a rampage.

Oh great, what now?

He stepped into his bedroom and sank onto the end of his bed. Whatever it was, it was sure to be his fault.

He stared at his bedroom door, hearing loud thumps of footsteps pounding up the stairs towards his room.

What is it this time? Did I accidently help an old lady across the street and embarrass my mother again?

He slumped his shoulders while sighing. He tried to be evil, he did, but on some level, he knew that his parents were right. Nice people did get fucked over in this dimension, but an integral part of him refused to allow him to cheat and hurt other demons. It just wasn't fair. He tried really hard, but demons that didn't seem to try at all found evil so easy.

I'm cursed, that's what it is. Some dark fairy has put a conscience on me, so I'll be cursed for all eternity.

He knew that wasn't true, but there was something wrong with him. Everyone told him there was, so it must be true.

They mocked his looks. He wasn't dark and seedy like he should be. He had golden hair and blue eyes. He wasn't twisted and scary. He looked like a human!

His mother had made him have many tests as a child to find out why his skin was tawny. When he developed muscles in his shoulders and chest, she'd had him sent to an institution to check him for humanity diseases. They hadn't found anything in his genes, so she'd bought him cloaks to cover him up, and hats with horns on. When his horns had eventually grown in, she'd been appalled that they only appeared when he was angry.

He sighed. And his father—

He yelped as his door flew open and a giant, scaly black demon burst into the room. Its arms were as thick as tree trunks, and there were black veins popping up in its neck.

It flashed its gigantic black wings, its red eyes locked on him in a menacing stare.

"What are you—?"

Kieron didn't finish as the demon rushed forwards and grabbed him by the neck, lifting him up off the bed and holding him elevated by the throat.

"What did you do?" It bellowed, blasting torrid air in his face.

Kieron gasped for air, trying to wrestle the sharp talons from around his neck. He tried to speak, but the giant claws wrapped around his throat were blocking it.

"Put him down." He heard his mother's voice behind the demon. Green smoke filled the doorway before she appeared through the mist and stepped into the room.

"Oh, I'll put him down alright, like the mongrel he is." The black demon snarled in Kieron's face, its long fangs glinting at him as saliva dripped down them.

"Lionel." Kieron heard his mother growl with menace in her tone.

The demon narrowed its red eyes at him as it squeezed his throat even tighter.

Kieron gasped, trying to inhale.

My father, the badass demon lord. He narrowed his eyes at the demon in retaliation.

"Put him down, NOW!" His mother screamed as one of her vine-like green tendrils smacked his father on the back of the head.

The black demon grumbled, releasing his grip on Kieron and dropping him onto his bed. Then he rubbed the back of his head and turned to face his mother.

"The little shit deserves it. Look what he's done!" His father whined.

"So that's an excuse for you to demon-out and kill him. Put your goddamn face back on, and do try to be respectable."

Kieron watched his mother shake her head, and her green tendrils faded away, leaving the visage of a prim brunette wearing an apron.

His father growled, and then transformed into his human form. His black scaly body shrank into that of a debonair dark-haired man in his forties.

"You need to learn to control your temper," Kieron's mother muttered as she stepped past his father and smiled at Kieron.

"You need to learn to control your offspring," his father mumbled under his breath.

"What's going on?" Kieron sat up, rubbing his neck.

"You're going on a trip." His mother's smile never reached her eyes. "It'll be an adventure."

Kieron shuddered at the crazy gleam in her eyes. "What kind of trip?" He backed up on the bed as she hovered over him.

26

"One that will make you into a real fucking demon, rather than a wet human," his father roared at him.

"Lionel, please!" His mother's head spun around as she glared at his father.

"Well it's true. It's about time he demoned-up. He can't cling to your apron strings forever."

Kieron felt a shiver of fear. He'd never been anywhere but here before. This was all he knew.

"W-where am I going?" He shuddered at the thought of going somewhere even worse, but there was a glimmer of hope that he'd be going somewhere better.

Where else could be worse?

"You should be asking *why* you're going." His father narrowed his eyes.

Kieron glanced at his mother. She smiled as she kicked back, hitting his father squarely on the kneecap.

"Oww, fuck!" His father hopped on one leg, hugging his knee.

"Your results on the pure evil examination were a little low, so you're going to a kind of training camp. You'll be okay though. You just need to really embrace evil this time, okay?" His mother said softly, but the ice in her eyes left no doubt in his mind that it was an order.

"A little low? He failed so badly, the examiner was pissing himself laughing!" His father shouted.

Kieron watched his mother's eyes narrow, and her nostrils flared as she spun around to face his father.

His father's already pale skin visibly lightened as the blood drained out of his face. "Okay, okay. I'm done." He held up his hands in surrender.

"Er, what kind of training camp?" Kieron asked. He had a suspicion that he wasn't going to like the answer.

"It's called the Claws dimension," his mother said. "They're sending you a portal to it today. You'll be fine." She smiled at him over her shoulder, but the smile was icy cold.

"Dad?" Kieron widened his eyes. Another dimension would be impossible to return from. He hadn't even started portal training yet.

His father shrugged. "I tried, son. You're screwed and—"

His mother slapped his father across the face. "Stop scaring him!"

Kieron shivered. His father was evil, but at least he didn't keep secrets like his mother did. He jumped when the onyx walls of his room began to shimmer, and a blast of wind howled through the room.

"That'll be your ride." He barely heard his mother's voice over the rush of wind caused by the circular hole that appeared in his hellish reality.

"Noooo!" he cried as the gusts tugged on his body, pulling him towards the gaping hole in the room, sucking him towards it.

"Mom, dad, please!" He clawed at his bed as he was dragged off it and sucked into the portal. "Help me!"

He saw his father shake his head. "Learn from it, and do try to survive," he shouted over the noise.

Kieron screamed as his body was sucked into the portal, and his world faded away into the distance.

29

JINGLE BELLS

K ieron cried out as he fell helplessly down the dark tunnel of the portal towards a blinding white light beneath him. Echoes of other worlds and other dimensions flashed past his eyes as he sped by them at high speed.

He swallowed hard, his heart racing. He tried to steel himself for landing in another world, but his body shook at the thought. Hell was all he knew. He'd never even been in a portal before.

Bile rose as his body was battered from one side of the portal tunnel to the other, but he managed to hold back the urge to throw up.

His eyes widened as the white light grew in size while he fell towards it. It glowed with almost holy light. He tried to claw at the sides of the tunnel to slow his descent, but they were smooth like glass, and he just slid down them through the opening instead.

He dropped onto an ice-cold pile of white dust, flopping face first into the wet flakes. He lifted his head to see white powder explode around him, and blinked the melting snow out of his eyes.

Is this where Hell freezes over?

He peered around at the winter wonderland with wide eyes. The landscape was a blanket of snow that appeared to stretch for miles ahead of him up to a mountainous region. The blue skies above were lit up by bright sunshine.

He rolled over, his teeth chattering. His red t-shirt was cold and wet as it clung to his chest and back. He jumped up out of the snow and rubbed his bare arms as a gust of icy wind blew against him.

I'm going to freeze to death.

He spun around, sighing when he saw the ragged entrance to a cave behind him. He hurried towards it, hoping to find refuge inside. His feet dragged through the snow, which quickly seeped into his sneakers and soaked the legs of his jeans.

His pulse raced when he tried to brush back his wet hair, only to find that the strands were already freezing into sharp spikes.

Just get to the cave.

He gritted his chattering teeth, and forced his body to move faster. The faster he could make a fire, the longer he would survive.

He dragged his legs through the snow as he neared the entrance to the cave.

Just a few more steps.

He paused when he heard a snorting sound coming from inside the cave. He listened for a moment, but the only sound came from the cold wind that was cutting across his skin in spikes of ice. He shook his head as he hurried through the cavernous entrance.

It was pitch black inside the chamber, so he rubbed his hands before casting a spell for light and warmth.

"Incinderai," he mumbled while holding out his hands. A small globe containing fire appeared in his hands. The outside of the globe was warm in his fingers as he scanned the small chamber, using it like a torch.

The craggy cave had several jutting out ledges and a small central floor with dark tunnels leading off from it.

He walked to the center of the chamber and put the globe in the middle of the floor before it burnt his hands as it began to heat up. He sighed and stood in front of the fiery globe, feeling the warmth of it growing and heating the cave. The light it gave off also increased, illuminating the dark corners.

He sighed and sat down beside the fire, trying to dry his clothes.

He jumped when there was a snorting sound behind him and spun around to find a giant pair of bloodshot brown eyes staring at him, just inches from his face.

He yelped and scrambled backwards as he noticed a long brown snout below the eyes, with razor-sharp fangs poking out of the creature's mouth.

Black antlers rose up from its skull into deadly looking points that scratched the roof of the cave as it shook its head and snorted smoke out of its nostrils. It growled at Kieron, stamping its cloven feet on the ground and shaking its head at him as if it were about to charge.

What the fuck is that thing?

The monster's thick brown fur shook on its long body as it narrowed its eyes at Kieron.

He tried to think of a spell to ward it off, but his mind emptied when its eyes crossed and its thick pink tongue lolled out of its mouth. It looked like a gigantic retarded deer.

It snarled and banged it's hooves on the floor before charging at him. The little bells around its neck jingled merrily as it plowed towards him.

"Phobious!" Kieron cried on instinct, pushing both his hands out towards the creature. Blue light shot from his fingers and hit the animal squarely between the eyes. It flopped backwards onto its ass and shook its head.

Kieron shook his head.

I can't believe I used the phobia spell on a fucked up deer. What exactly is it going to be scared of?

He warily stood up and walked towards the creature, watching its crossed eyes widen in horror as he drew nearer. It neighed and jumped to its feet before turning and galloping out of the cave at full speed. He frowned and watched it bound across the untouched snow until it faded into the distance.

I guess I made it scared of me.

"What the fuck was that anyway?" he muttered as he turned and sat beside the fire once more.

"It was a reindeer," a female voice said behind him.

He spun around to see a pretty blonde girl standing in the entrance of the cave.

"May I?" she asked, pointing to the fire.

"Oh, uh, sure." He jumped to his feet and waved her into the cave.

He couldn't help but notice her shapely legs as she hurried out of the storm and into the cave. She wore fur-lined snow boots, a thickly padded white jacket and skin-tight blue jeans.

"He won't be happy that you've hurt one of his pets." She shot him a mischievous grin, her blue eyes sparkling with amusement.

"Wait, that monstrosity was someone's pet?"

"It's one of his herd." She warmed her hands over the fire before sitting cross-legged in front of it and pushing the fur hood off her head to reveal a tumble of blonde curls and two dark horns pointing through the top of her head.

Is she a demon like me?

He took a seat beside her, studying her with interest. She was a very pretty demon.

"Who's herd?" he asked, already starting to like his new companion.

She turned to him, frowning with an amused glint of disbelief in her eyes. "Satan Claws, of course."

5

PRACTICE MAKES PERFECT

"Don't be silly, Satan Claws isn't real," Kieron laughed. "He's just a warning story for Hell spawn during the winter."

The girl frowned at him. "You're not from this realm, are you?"

"No, I'm here for a kind of training camp," he said. "I'm from Hell."

"Ohh." She nodded. "You're one of those demons."

"What does that mean? What kind of demon are you?" He studied the pale blue gloves on her hands, frowning. They were skin-tight.

She flexed her fingers, and he noticed that her

claws were on the outside of her gloves.

"I'm a succubus." She offered him her hand. "My name's Leila."

He took her hand and shook it. When he felt how warm her hands were, he realized that the gloves were not gloves at all. A soft pale blue fur covered her skin. "I'm er, Kieron." He smiled, wondering if the soft blue fur covered her entire body. It felt nice and silky. He peered up at her face. There was no fur there.

Maybe it's just on her hands.

"I meant that you're not the first demon to be sent here for failing evil." She glanced at him.

"Oh." He looked away, embarrassed that she knew how lame he was. "Yeah, I keep trying to get better at it."

"At least you're not stuck here." She smiled.

"Are you from here?"

She shook her head. "No, I'm from Hell too, but I kinda got exiled here. And trust me when I say that Satan Claws is very real in this dimension."

He shook his head. "Come on, you're messing with me, right? There's a big evil fat guy who breaks into demon spawn's houses and bankrupts their parents?" He laughed. "Even I'm not that naïve."

"He does a hell of a lot more than that. He's got an army of minions and bombs disguised as trees, man. I've seen him wreak havoc on the people here. It's the darkest magic when he casts his spells."

Kieron stood up, still shaking his head as he brushed the dust off the back of his jeans. "So, I'm supposed to learn evil from Satan Claws? Yeah, right."

"Nah, I think you're supposed to get instructions. It's been different for all of the demons that got sent here." Leila pointed to a dark corner in the cave. "They always talk to their mentors on those things."

He turned and peered into the shadowed corner of the cave. After a moment, he noticed a small altar with a summoning bowl on it.

He walked over to the bowl and peered inside it. It was dusty and empty. "You've known a lot of the demons that come here, then?" He glanced back at her.

A seductive smile appeared on her pouty pink lips. "I'm drawn to them, succubus remember."

He felt a grin form on his face. Stuck in a cave with a hot demon girl, it could be worse. "I guess I better find out what my mentor has to say." He winked.

"Good luck."

He shivered as he looked down into the summoning bowl. He probably needed luck. His mentor could be anyone.

Gritting his teeth, he picked up the jar of powder beside the bowl and sprinkled it into the dish. Next, he picked up the scroll and read it. The location of his caller would be listed in the spell. He frowned at the old parchment.

My mentor is a rotted soul?

He shrugged and read the spell.

"CALLING INTO THE DARKNESS,
CONNECT ME WITH A ROTTED SOUL,
MAKE MY ENEMIES CLAWLESS,
AND SEND MY VOICE INTO THIS BOWL."

He waited, watching the red dust swirl inside the

bowl in a circular motion. Sparks of fire flared up on each speck, creating a cosmos of tiny spinning stars. The little glowing embers merged to create glowing numbers in a circular dial around the edges of the dish.

He frowned at them. He'd never seen a communication spell do that before.

There was a ringing in his ears as the ground shook. The ringing became more insistent as he waited for someone to answer his call.

Come on, come on. Answer the goddamn call.

He tapped his fingers impatiently on the altar, becoming increasingly irritated by the blaring rings in his head.

There was a loud click, and the constant ringing abated. He breathed a sigh of relief and listened to the voice.

"Welcome to the examinations board. Please listen to the following question and think carefully before answering," a seductive female voice said.

He frowned.

More tests, what the hell?

He shook his head and listened for further

instructions.

"If you wish to speak about your exam results, but only have two nouns and an adverb in your available vocabulary, please smash your head into a wall seventeen times, and then press one."

He shook his head. Who'd be stupid enough to do that?

Someone with only three words in their vocabulary, he answered himself. He listened for the next option, quickly discovering he had missed half of it while he was considering the first one, so he only caught the last part of it.

"... And then shove it up your ass," the voice said.

Hopefully that wasn't my option.

"If you would like to speak to your mentor because you failed so miserably at your examination that we sent you to stupid camp, then please press three. You also might want to consider bending over and kissing your ass goodbye."

Stupid camp? Oh fucking great! I'm not bending over and kissing anything.

He peered at the glowing embers that formed the number three in the bowl. He really didn't want to touch fire, but he didn't have a choice. He pressed number three, yelping when the embers of hot dust burnt the tip of his finger.

"Lascher, is that your girl-like scream I hear?" Kieron groaned when he recognized the voice on the other end of the line. "Congratulations on surviving your arrival. I expected you to drown in the snow upon your arrival because you were hugging it better." Kazaik's voice was unusually cheerful for once.

"You're my mentor?" Kieron blurted. It was bad enough being stuck in stupid camp, but with Kazaik as his mentor, he was certain to be trapped here for eternity.

"Aww, don't get sentimental on me now, Lascher. I'm supposed to be toughening that gentle hide of yours up," Kazaik said. "If that's even possible." He heard the professor mutter under his breath.

"What do I need to do?" he asked, clenching his hands into fists. This was going to suck. Kazaik wouldn't want him to come back to Hell, so he wasn't going to be any help.

"Isn't it obvious by now?" Kazaik's sarcastic tone

caused Kieron's blood to boil.

Kieron glanced around the cave. Leila waved at him from her place by the fire. "Not really," he muttered.

"Learn to be evil, Lascher, you fucking moron!" the professor snapped back.

"Is that it?" Kieron shook his head. It was a bit vague for an instruction.

"Well." Kazaik sighed. "There are some ground rules. First, you need to practice. I'm sure there are some nice people for you to mess with over there. There's a whole village of them to choose from, from what I gather. After that you just—"

Kieron winced as loud crackles of static echoed in his ears. "What? I can't hear you!"

"—and then destroy the master of the realm."

"Wait, destroy who? I couldn't hear you."

"I'm not obliged to repeat it, regardless of how deaf you are." Kazaik laughed before he disconnected the call.

"Wait, that's not fair," Kieron cried, but the professor had already gone, and the embers had turned black.

"Son of a bitch!" He knocked over the bowl. He was certain the professor had caused the crackling on purpose.

He sighed and turned to find Leila standing behind him with a look of concern on her face.

"What happened?" she asked.

"He made it so I couldn't hear what I'm supposed to do. I'm screwed."

"What did you hear? Maybe I can help."

"He told me to practice being evil, and then destroy the master of the realm."

"Oh, that's easy. I know who the master of the realm is."

"Who?" A spark of hope lit up inside him.

"Satan Claws."

The spark fizzled out when he heard that. "You're kidding, right?

She shook her head, and her blonde curls swished around her head. "Seriously, he's the master here, but there's only one thing that can destroy him."

"What's that?" He didn't even believe in the guy. How was he supposed to destroy him, with wishes and moonbeams?

45

"The Weaver Codex."

Kieron narrowed his eyes at Leila. For all he knew, she was stringing him along too. He'd heard of the codex, but doubted it was outside of Hell. It was one of the most powerful artifacts in Hell, a scroll with the power of the universe contained within it.

"Why are you trapped here for eternity Leila?"

She lowered her dark lashes as she stared at her feet. "I committed the worst crime in Hell."

"You called the Devil fugly?" He widened his eyes.

"No. Okay, the second worst." She lifted her blue eyes to meet his. "I fell in love." She shook her head. "It was stupid. I should have known better."

"That's a crime?" He frowned. He was sure love was allowed, or at least a version of it.

"It is for succubae," she muttered. Then she smiled. "Hey, I have an idea."

He shot her a questioning look.

"You need to get to the codex and destroy Satan Claws, and I need to get out of here. How about, I help you find them, and you use the codex to take me back to Hell with you?"

46

"We don't even know for certain that I'm supposed to destroy him." Ignoring the fact that he was convinced Satan Claws didn't exist, he found the idea of destroying someone repulsive. "Also…" He peered at his feet. "I'm er, not very good at evil."

"It has to be him. There isn't anyone else here who could be the master of this realm." She shrugged. "And I know where he and the codex are. Plus, I can teach you evil, or at least how to bullshit your way through it."

He considered his options. He didn't have any other ideas. He did like the sound of being able to bullshit his way through being evil. "Okay, why not." He nodded. "Where are they?"

She smiled brightly. "The grotto."

"Oh, you've gotta be fucking kidding me."

6

THE CUTENESS WILL KILL YOU

Kieron peered at the brightly lit village with
narrowed eyes as icy sleet sliced across the
skin on his face. He pulled the fur hood
down over his face and dragged his boots through the
snow, thankful that his magic still worked here.
Without it, he'd still be wearing sneakers and a t-shirt.

"You okay?" Leila shouted over the loud gales
that were battering against them both.

"It's fucking freezing!" he cried back.

"We'll warm up in the village. Hurry up." She
turned to face the village and hunched forwards as
she plowed her boots through the snow, heading
towards the small buildings at a faster speed.

He followed her, dragging his feet as he sighed at

the colorful village. The houses were quaint, little cottages with bright lights decorating them. There were brightly colored decorations on snowy lawns where happy children dressed in colorful clothes were making snowmen and playing.

A part of him didn't want to go to the village because he knew when he got there that he had to practice evil. The people looked happy. It was the last place he wanted to be evil.

Leila turned back to face him. "Come on!"

He shook his head. He had to, didn't he? He gritted his teeth and hurried through the snow.

This is going to suck.

As they entered the village, a bright red and green sign lit up with a smiley face and the words, 'Welcome to Christletown'.

Oh great, even the signs are happy.

He passed a small child wearing a bright red parka. The child was smiling as he licked a giant lollipop. When the little boy waved at him, he limply waved back.

This is going to really suck!

The gales abated as they entered the village, and

the small cottages blocked the wind. He wiped the snow off his face with gloved hands, breathing easy for a moment.

Jingly music came from a small band that was playing on a makeshift stage in the center of the village. Crowds of people stood around the stage while eating baked goods and cheering at the music.

Kieron hurried to catch up with Leila. "Where are we going?"

She brushed back her hood, and her golden hair fell out of it and down her back. "Let's go into the inn and get some hot cider. It'll warm us up." She smiled.

"Okay." He nodded, trying to smile, but the sense of foreboding in the pit of his stomach was making him feel ill.

As they entered a small rustic inn, the sounds of people gaily chatting caused his stomach to flip over.

How can I practice evil here? It'd be like shooting a puppy.

He blinked when he noticed that the people around the bar all had oddly shaped ears. He spun around and peered at the patrons of the inn.

From families eating food, to the old man perched at the bar, everyone seemed small and had weird pointy ears.

He gripped Leila's arm and pulled her closer to him. "Hey," he whispered in her ear. "What's wrong with these people?"

She frowned. "Nothing, what do you mean?"

"They're all so little, and look at their ears."

"They're perfectly normal elves," she said as she unzipped her jacket and hung it on the coat stand beside her.

He widened his eyes. "They're all elves?"

"Yeah." She shrugged as if he should know that before turning and walking towards an empty booth at the back of the inn.

He gritted his teeth and unzipped his jacket.

Great, I have to be evil to a cute, little elf.

He shrugged out of his sodden parka and hung it on the coat stand. Then he turned around to face Leila.

He glanced down at his feet, feeling ashamed, but instead of seeing his boots, he saw a pair of wide green eyes looking up at him. He stared at the teenage elf, her auburn locks curled around her cherubic face as she innocently looked up at him.

"What?" he asked, feeling uncomfortable under her wide-eyed gaze.

"Are you an angel?" she asked.

"Er, no." He self-consciously brushed back his blond bangs and attempted to look mean.

"You look like one," she said as her pouty pink lips broke into a bright smile.

"I er, don't," he grumbled, trying to sound mean.

She beckoned him to come closer, gesturing with her hand.

He sighed and leaned forwards, so that she could whisper in his ear.

"Don't be sad, mister. Even in the worst of times, things always get better." Her breath smelled like cotton candy.

He stood up straight, frowning down at her. He wanted to tell her what a crock of shit that was, but she looked so sweet that he didn't have the heart to do it. He smiled and nodded instead.

She hugged his waist before turning on her heel and running back to her table.

I'm so screwed.

He walked over to Leila, taking a seat opposite her. "I can't do it."

She sipped her hot cider, shooting him a questioning look. "Can't do what?"

"I can't practice evil here."

"Why not? There are tons of opportunities." She scanned the inn with narrowed eyes.

"They're cute, adorable elves. I can't do it," he snapped.

"Well, it's them or me because there's no one else here." She shrugged.

"What about the bullshit? Can't we bullshit our way out of it?"

She studied her drink for a moment. "The thing is, you're kind of easy to read. I dunno if you can pull it off."

"Can't we at least try? Teach me to be hard to read."

She rolled up the sleeves of her pink jumper, revealing blue furred arms. "Okay, well, we can try." She nodded.

"Right, what do I need to do first?" he asked,

hopeful that he could escape the fate of harming the cute elves.

"Well, my talent is seduction. If you can seduce someone, you can make them do or believe anything, so I'm going to teach you to seduce people."

"Er, that'll only work on girls, won't it?" He shifted uncomfortably in his seat.

"Nah, it's an equal opportunity world out there. What are you, from the dark ages?"

"You want me to seduce Kazaik?" He wrinkled his nose up at the thought.

"You just have to seduce the system. As long as you can convince the evil-bot that you're evil, we're outta here."

"What the fuck is the evil-bot?"

She rolled her eyes. I can't believe demons don't know this. Okay, it's an automated algorithm, which decides evil levels for examinations. It runs through all the test results and ticks the ones that hit a certain level. You think your mentor gets off his ass and checks all the tests." She shook her head. "Nah, the results are sent to him from evil-bot. It's all automated, man."

"So, I er, have to seduce evil-bot? How the hell do I do that?"

"If I knew that, do you think I'd still be here? But I bet that the codex would help. I mean, I can tell you what evil-bot responds to, but it's pretty complex."

"Can't I just tell it that is looks pretty?" he asked.

She laughed. "Well, it never hurts to compliment it on its curvy data storage."

"Okay then, we need to get into the grotto, get the codex, destroy Satan Claws and seduce evil-bot?" He sighed. "How do we get into the grotto? Assuming the codex is there, Satan Claws isn't a figment of your imagination, and I can seduce a robot."

"We walk in," she said before taking a sip of her drink.

He sat back in his chair and studied her. "You don't sweat the small stuff, do you?"

"Why worry about what might be?" She offered him a sly smile and winked.

"Fair point. Satan's Grotto, here we come then." He frowned as he stared out of the frosted window with worry knotting in his stomach.

55

7

SATAN'S GROTTO

Kieron stared around the grotto with wide eyes. Elves were chained to various workstations across the room. Unlike the happy elves from Christletown village, these ones were scraggy and thin with dark hollows under their eyes. They didn't smile as they worked on building weapons for their dark master.

He focused on the nearest elf, a small girl, who was wearing a dirty, torn rag as a dress. She glanced up at him with sad eyes before quickly going back to assembling an M16.

"Come on," Leila said, interrupting the pure horror he felt at the scene before him. "We don't have time to watch the elves work. We need to find the codex."

"Work, they chose to do this?" He frowned as an ogre in a guard's uniform walked behind an elderly elf and lashed his back with whip before ordering him to work faster.

"Well, no, but that's not really our problem," Leila said before she grabbed his arm and pulled him through an open doorway to their left.

He stared back into the main hall of the grotto, feeling a range of emotions, and none of them were good.

"Can't we help them?" he asked.

She turned and frowned at him. "You're the weirdest demon I've ever met." She shook her head. "We need to help ourselves." She turned on her heel and hurried down the dark corridor.

He knew she was right, but the urge to help the little elves was so strong. He frowned as he hurried after her.

Maybe there is something wrong with me.

He was a demon. He was supposed to enjoy the suffering of others, but instead he had a horrible feeling in the pit of his stomach at the thought of the enslaved elves.

Shaking his head at the insanity of a caring demon, he glanced down the corridor. The walls were dirty granite with shadowy stains on them. The stone beneath his feet was slimy and slippery with moss growing in the many cracks.

He glanced up at Leila's slim back. Her puffy jacket clung to her curves down to her jean-clad hips.

"Do you know where you're going?" he whispered.

"Yeah, I think so." She paused at the door to her left. I think the codex is in here, but I heard it was guarded." She pointed to the closed door.

He stared at the thick metal door. It was rusty and old, but it looked unbreakable.

"Guarded by what?" he asked as he reached for the handle. It turned with a loud creak that made him wince. He pushed open the door and stared into the room.

"That," she whispered as she pointed to the giant, furry beast ahead of them.

Curled up and sleeping on a frayed rug in the center of the room was a fluffy dragon. It was covered in thick silver fur, but judging by the shape of its head and its long forked tail, it was definitely a dragon.

At the back of the room, behind the sleeping monster was a glass case with a scroll inside it.

That must be the codex.

A blast of warm air hit him as the creature blasted out a loud snore. He silently studied it for a moment before gesturing for Leila to be quiet and follow him.

Hitching his breath, he tiptoed around the sleeping dragon, taking care not to make a sound.

He glanced back at Leila to find her doing the same.

He paused when he came to the creature's thick tail, which was swishing up and down in spasmodic movements, like that of an angry cat.

He glanced at the creature, noticing its sharp claws digging into the rug. Green slime dripped onto its claws. He glanced up to the dragon's head, noticing green saliva drooling from its mouth and rolling down its fangs, which were poking out over its bottom lip. The liquid dripped off the point of its fangs onto its claws.

Dragons could kill demons. He knew they were

the only creature that could kill him, and not just slash him up a bit. They could destroy a demon in a way that it never came back. He shivered as fear shot down his spine.

Don't think about it. Just get the codex, and get out of here.

He watched the rhythmic swishing of the furred tail, counting the seconds on when it went up and when it went down. After a beat, he jumped over the tail, passing it as it swished downwards.

Turning to face Leila, he saw fear in her eyes. He silently gestured for her to do the same.

She stubbornly shook her head.

"Come on," he whispered.

"Not a chance. I'll wait here," she whispered back, stubbornly folding her arms.

He sighed. "Fine."

Turning to face the codex, he hurried past the dragon. He rushed over to the glass case and quickly lifted it up, snatching up the scroll inside it. He peered at the scroll, his eyes widening. This was it. This was the codex.

He shoved the scroll into the back pocket of his

jeans and hurried back to Leila.

The dragon's tail still swished up and down, so he gestured for her to step back as he prepared to leap over it again.

His pulse was racing.

Come on, we're nearly out of here.

Leila backed up, and he leapt over the tail again, but this time his foot caught on the fluffy end of it. He landed safely beside Leila, but quickly glanced at the sleeping beast, fearing he'd touched it.

Its claws still dug into the rug. Slime still dripped from its fangs. He stared at its closed eyes, and nearly screamed when one green eye slid open and stared at him.

He froze on the spot, trying to breathe through a blocked throat. He could feel Leila tightly gripping his arm, but couldn't look away from the creature's open eye.

The floor vibrated as a low growl rumbled through the room, and the dragon raised itself up onto all fours, both eyes now staring at him and Leila.

"Run!" Leila cried.

"No, wait." He managed as he heard the jingle of

61

bells and noticed a bright red collar with a bell on it around the dragon's neck. "It's a pet, not a guard."

The dragon snarled and hunched over. Its large, muscled shoulders trembled in preparation to attack.

"I don't care if it's a fucking pet. I don't want to be dragon kibble." She tugged on his arm, trying to pull him towards the doorway.

"I've got an idea." He smiled and glanced at the fur-lined hood hanging from Leila's collar. "Give me your hood."

"What?" She widened her eyes at him.

"Just, trust me. It'll work. I'm sure of it."

She shook her head as she quickly unzipped the fluffy hood, detaching it from her jacket before handing it to him.

He pushed the hood inside out, and then rolled it into a ball before waving it at the dragon. "Here boy."

The narrowed green eyes of the creature widened as they focused on the hood. It tilted its head sideways and sat down, following the movement of the fluffy ball in Kieron's hand.

"Oh, you've gotta be kidding me," Leila

muttered.

"You want it, boy, do ya?" Kieron jerked the fluffy ball in fake throws.

The dragon's eyes followed the fluff, darting back and forth while Kieron shook the ball at it. It hunched playfully on the rug, watching the Kieron's hands as he teased the creature.

Kieron flung the ball to the back of the room. "Go get it, boy!"

The dragon bounded after the ball of fluff and leapt onto it, making the room shake. Its teeth ripped into it as it boosted the hood around the room, and then chased it.

"Let's go." Kieron grabbed Leila's hand and pulled her out of the room, quickly shutting the door behind him. He rested against the closed door and sighed.

"That was just ridiculous," Leila muttered as she folded her arms. "How did you know it would chase my hood?"

"If you put a collar with a bell on something, it has to enjoy play time." He shrugged. "If not, it wouldn't let you put a collar on it."

CLAIRE CHILTON

She frowned for a moment. "Yeah, that even works for BDSM." She nodded.

He widened his eyes. He'd meant puppies, not sex kittens.

He shook his head, trying to ignore the sexual thoughts in his mind and focus on their mission instead. "What now?"

"We need to find out how to use the codex to take out Satan Claws."

"Okay." He pulled the scroll out of his back pocket and read it. It was in Latin, of course.

He frowned at the scroll. "There's only one spell in here."

"What does it do?"

"Anything I want."

"That's easy then. Wish Claws dead. You'll pass evil, and we can both go home."

He frowned. "How do I take you back with me if I only have one spell?"

"Oh …" She narrowed her eyes. "Crap. What about if you wish us both back to Hell?"

He shook his head. "That won't work. I'll still fail evil and be sent back here. We need to think of

64

something that will fix both problems." In the back of his mind, there were three problems. The elves needed his help, but he didn't tell Leila that.

"Let's find out where Satan Claws is. Maybe the solution will come to us?" she said. "It beats standing around here anyway."

He nodded, gesturing for her to lead the way. She seemed to know her way around the grotto.

She turned and continued walking down the corridor.

He followed her in silence for a few minutes as they headed deeper into the grotto. The stone walls became a cavernous tunnel made from dark granite. It reminded him of the punishment sector in Hell.

"Er Leila, how long have you been stuck here for?" He eventually broke the silence.

"A couple of hundred years," she said, glancing over her shoulder at him.

"Wow, that's a long time to be stuck here. You seem to have survived okay though."

"Yeah, the elves helped me. I'd have been Satan Claws' bitch if they hadn't hidden me."

"Why do you want to go back to Hell? I mean, if

we kill Satan claws, won't this be a nice place? It's not as if Hell was very nice to you."

"I need to save Dorian. He was imprisoned before they exiled me. I made a promise to go back and get him." Her voice darkened with seriousness for the first time, and they both fell silent for a moment.

"Why do you want to go back?" she asked in a brighter voice. "It's not as if Hell was very nice to you either."

He thought about it for a moment. What did Hell have to offer him? He frowned while he tried to think of one thing that he had to go back for, but there wasn't much about Hell that he liked. "My mother will come and get me, and kill me many times if I don't go home," he muttered. It didn't matter what he wanted. He knew his mother well enough to know that a little realm displacement wouldn't stop her kicking his ass if he failed again.

She came to a stop and spun around to face him with wide eyes. "That's not a good reason to go back."

He shrugged. "I'm a demon lord. Where else am I going to belong? Anyway, I like it hot. It's too cold here."

She shook her head. "The weather, that's your reason? Seriously, you need to find something in the world that you love."

"Maybe I will, one day," he muttered while peering at his feet.

"I hope you do," she said with a smile before turning and continuing down the tunnel.

I hope so too.

They came to a halt outside a massive wooden doorway. He glanced up at the double doors that were at least twelve feet high, then peered at Leila. "He's in here?"

She squinted up at the doors with a grimace. "Yeah, I think so. Have you come up with any ideas on what spell to use yet?"

He really didn't have a clue what to do, but he had his own magic on his side. Surely one of the spells would work. There wasn't a choice. This was the only way to get home.

He shivered as a cold draft blew down the tunnel. Getting here had seemed like the most important thing, but now he was here, he really didn't want to open the door.

"Well?" she asked.

"Er yeah, I have a plan," he muttered.

"What is it?"

"I'm still working out the finer details."

She narrowed her eyes at him.

"Just um, stay back, and don't do anything dangerous." He gripped the handle of the door and turned it. The old lock grinded loudly before clicking open. He pushed the door wide and stepped into the room.

A giant ogre was seated on a thorny metal throne, its bulky weight covered in thick armor. It turned to stare at them before expelling a hollow laugh.

"Food that delivers itself!" It roared as it patted its belly. "I love my world." It grinned at Kieron, and licked its lips.

He turned to Leila. "It eats demons," he hissed.

"It eats anything," she muttered.

"Great!"

8

SATAN CLAWS

Kieron pushed Leila behind him in a protective motion. Then he turned to face the ogre. "Satan Claws, I presume?"

"Oh, I love it when groupies drop by. No wait, I don't. I hope you don't taste like fawning bitch." He eyed Kieron with curiosity. "Still, a bit of hot sauce, and anything tastes good."

"Don't you think you've eaten enough?" Kieron asked, pointedly eyeing his bulging belly.

"I'm big boned." Satan Claws snarled at him.

"Yeah, I noticed." Kieron tried to work out how to handle this, but he had to destroy this guy. That was why he was here, right? An unsettling feeling of discomfort washed over him.

What if he's not actually the bad guy? I mean, okay he eats a lot of people, but that's not a crime is it? Maybe they want to be eaten.

He decided to try to find out what was real and what was not. All he knew about Satan Claws was a bedtime story, after all. "So you eat demons?" he asked.

"And elves, and people, and small puppies." The ogre nodded.

"Right. Would you say that was against their will?"

"What the hell kind of dipshit are you? No, they willingly jumped onto my plate." Satan Claws shot him an incredulous glance.

"Okay, so you kill the innocent. Right, I can work with that. Thanks for clarifying it." He smiled politely.

He's bad. I need to kill him.

"Clarifying what?" The ogre leaned forwards in his chair, frowning at him.

"Well, that you're bad. I only know myth, but facts are much more reliable, don't you think?"

"I'm the darkest, baddest bitch in all the universe!"

Satan Claws sat up in his chair and stuck out his chin.

"Oh yeah, what other stuff do you do?" Kieron asked.

"I make the elves work until they die, then I eat their remains. Sometimes, I eat them before then."

"Yeah, that's pretty evil." Kieron nodded. "You're only the most evil in this realm though. I mean technically, the universe has many realms in it."

"And I go to them!" Satan Claws bellowed as he stood up and stomped over to Kieron and Leila. "I go to Earth and steal presents from children in the winter. I bankrupt their parents during they're stupid holidays. I am the monster that lurks in their closet at night and haunts their dreams. That is the reality for you, tiny demon!"

"I see." Kieron said as a smile spread across his face. He just figured out how to solve all of his problems with one spell. The answer was reality.

Satan Claws roared as he reached down and scooped Leila up into his giant fist. "And now, I'm going to kill your pretty little friend."

"Kieron, if you've got a plan, now is the time to use it!" she cried as she struggled in the grip of the giant ogre.

"Oh right, shit." Kieron reached into his back pocket and pulled out the scroll.

The ogre's eyes widened as he recognized it. "My codex!" He dropped Leila from his hands and reached for Kieron instead.

Leila landed on the cushioned throne, groaning as she rolled off it and scurried beneath it to hide.

Kieron rolled left and scrambled under the ogre's table, still gripping the scroll in his hands.

"It's mine!" Satan Claws roared as his giant fist smashed through the table top a few inches from Kieron's head.

Kieron scrambled back further, backing up against the wall as he quickly read the spell.

"Dark lords of space and time, make your ultimate power mine."

Shit, it's in Latin!

He quickly translated it, and said the spell again while concentrating on changing reality. All he could think of were the friendly-faced elves and their sparkly village. His body jolted as a green glow burned under his skin.

He stared down at his hands in horror as they lit up, and his skin heated up. The force of power flowing through his body was too strong. He screamed as it coursed through him.

The ogre flipped the table away from him and hovered over him. "Stupid demon snack, you just killed yourself." Its spittle hit his face as it grinned at him.

Kieron arched in agony, and the world exploded around him in flash of colorful lights.

When Kieron opened his eyes, he glanced up to see Leila's blue eyes staring at him. She poked him in the arm. "Are you alive?"

He sat up and rubbed his face. "I think I am. What happened, where's Satan Claws?"

"That's a weird thing to say. Have you worked out what to wish for yet?"

He sat up and a bout of dizziness hit him. He fought the urge to throw up and tried to concentrate on his surroundings. He was in a cheerful office, sitting on a plush red couch.

"Where are we?" He glanced around at the polished oak desk and array of wrapped gifts dotted around the room.

"Santa's office." She shrugged.

"You mean Satan Claws, he's still alive?" He shook his head, trying to work out what had gone wrong.

"Who?" she asked. Don't you remember? We came here to find Santa to ask for his help to go home." She frowned at him, brushing her blonde locks out of her face. "How hard did you hit your head?"

Kieron knew he'd changed reality, but it seemed he'd changed Leila's reality too. "And Santa is…?"

"Father Christmas, you know the jolly red fat guy who gives kids presents for Christmas."

"Right." Kieron nodded.

Oh shit, what did I do?

"He was invented by Coca Cola, come on. How can you not know this? Everyone knows who Santa is."

"Nope, it's coming back." He smiled, deciding that bullshitting himself out of trouble was his best option. "So the elves don't work here anymore?" he asked.

"Duh, of course they do. They work in the grotto."

His heart sank in his chest. It didn't work. They were still stuck here.

"Come on, I'll show you." She pulled him off the couch. "We need to go to the grotto anyway."

He reluctantly stood up and followed her out of the room. He'd failed. The elves were still slaves.

His eyes widened when he saw the grotto. It was bright with an array of toys being built by smiling elves, who wore bright green and red outfits as they constructed toys for children. "They look happy," he blurted.

"Yeah, well they're doing what they love," she muttered.

"But they're still slaves." He was confused. Why would they be happy?

"No, they're not. They're paid in candy canes and shit like that."

"Candy canes don't seem to be a very fair wage."

"They can go on strike if they don't like it." Leila

75

shrugged. "If people are happy in their shitty jobs, leave them alone."

He nodded. It was a better life for them. He'd done something right.

"Come on. We're going to be late for our meeting with Santa." She dragged him across the grotto towards a jolly fat man wearing a red suit, who was laughing while sitting on a red throne.

"That's Santa?" He eyed the man. With his white bushy beard, it was hard to recognize him as Satan Claws.

"Yeah, come on."

"What exactly am I supposed to do at this meeting?" Kieron refused to budge.

"Ask him to send us back to Hell!" she cried.

"Okay, okay. I'll ask." He shook his head. He'd saved the elves, and he might get Leila back to Hell, but there was no way he was going to pass the evil test. He eyed the cute reindeer as it munched on some hay. It looked oddly familiar as it crossed its eyes at him.

I'm so screwed.

He tentatively walked up to Santa, trying to smile.

"Hey there young man, come on over here, and tell me what you want for Christmas." The big fella patted his lap.

"What? I'm not sitting on your lap!" Kieron cried, appalled at the thought.

"You want your gift don't you? I can tell you've been a good boy this year." The jolly man smiled.

Kieron turned to grimace at Leila. She gestured for him to go towards Santa.

Closing his eyes for a moment at the humiliation of having to sit on a big, sweaty guy's lap, he swallowed before opening his eyes and walking over to Santa. He stared at the fat guy's lap, shaking his head. Then winced as he sat down.

"Tell me what you want for Christmas." The jolly man said as his arms encircled Kieron in a warm hug.

Not to be on your fucking lap right now.

"I want you to send Leila and I back to Hell, please. We want to go home." He narrowed his eyes at Leila, who was bent over laughing at his plight.

The big man shifted under him. "Okay son, you can go home. Now get up, you're a bit heavy," he groaned.

Kieron leapt off the man's lap and spun around. "We can go home now?"

"Yep, and Merry Christmas, ho ho ho!"

Kieron hurried over to Leila and stood beside her as a white light surrounded them both in a warm glow. "Did he just call me a ho?"

Leila burst out laughing again. "I dunno, but I will. You so sat on that guy's lap to get something from him, ho!"

The winter wonderland around them faded with little elves waving them on their way.

Kieron smiled at Leila. "Thanks for all your help."

She smiled back. "Thanks for getting me home. I hope your exams go okay."

"Me too," he muttered, wondering how he was going to avoid being sent to another camp when he got home.

"Hey, that's my stop." She pointed to the busy street that appeared in a portal beside them. She turned and gave Kieron a hug. "Keep in touch. You're my new best friend."

He hugged her back, feeling a warm glow spread through him as she turned and disappeared into the portal. He smiled as the glowing light traveled towards Castle Lascher. He'd just found something he liked in Hell, a best friend.

As the dark onyx walls of Castle Lascher became clearer, he gritted his teeth.

Assuming I get to stay in Hell after all this.

9

HELL'S REWARDS

K ieron stood on the front steps of Castle
Lascher, debating on whether to ring the bell
or just slip in using his keys.

*The chances are that no one even knows what I
did in the other realm.*

He eyed the sparkling Christmas lights that were
glinting from the windows of the castle. It seemed his
altered reality had traveled to Hell too. His home was
sparkling with Christmas cheer for the first time.

He allowed himself a proud smile for a moment.

I did this, and no one will ever know.

He unlocked the door with his keys and stepped
into the large foyer, scanning the sweeping staircase
for signs of his parents, but there was no one else

there.

There was soft music coming from the living room to his left. He turned towards it and walked up to the doorway, curious about what he would find there.

His mother and father were sitting on the couch, drinking what appeared to be eggnog. In front of them was a large green tree with sparkly decorations glinting on it and piles of presents beneath it.

What is this?

He stepped into the room and coughed to make his parents aware of his presence.

They both turned and beamed at him.

"Oh honey, you're here in time for the presents," his mother cried.

"Good timing, son. We were about to start without you."

Kieron frowned. "I've got presents?"

"Of course." His mother smiled and pointed to the tree. "It's Christmas and Santa has been."

Kieron eyed the gifts. "He leaves presents for people?"

"You know he does," his father said with a glint

of light in his dark eyes.

"Oh yeah, sure." Kieron nodded, wondering what other fucked up shit Santa did now.

He wandered over to the tree and studied the presents. His eyes widened when he noticed that the biggest pile of them were tagged with his name. "Are they all for me?" he gasped.

"What do you think?" His father must have stood up and walked over to him because his hot breath warmed the back of Kieron's neck.

Kieron turned to face his father with a bright smile on his face. Changing reality was fantastic. "It's amazing," he muttered.

"What's amazing is how fucking gullible you are," his father muttered as the glint of light in his eyes faded and they turned solid black with a murderous look appearing in them.

"What?" Kieron's pulse raced as he stared up at his father.

"You think changing reality will change Hell," his mother screamed. "You think that we don't know what you did?" She threw her glass of eggnog into the fire.

"I did evil things and came h-h-home." Kieron backed away from his father into the tree.

"You created a fat, jolly, moron who breaks into people's houses to *give* them gifts. It's all over the realms, even Earth! Of all the stupid—"

"One evil act, that's all you had to do." His mother interrupted. "Just one, but nooooo, you created happy fucking wonderland instead. I'll be a laughing stock at the next PTA meeting!"

Kieron gulped and stumbled away from the tree. "I didn't mean to—"

"To what!" his father cried as he threw his hands into the air and shot a fireball at the Christmas tree. "You didn't mean to make the darkest Pagan holiday into a tinsel-fest? You're going somewhere darker this time. Kazaik is on his way over."

"No, come on. I got out. A-a-and I did do something evil. I made something bad into something good. That's evil to the bad guy, right?"

"Actually, he's right." Kazaik's cold voice echoed through the room.

Kieron spun around to face his professor, surprised to hear him agree with him.

Kazaik took off his gloves and folded them neatly in his hands before continuing. "Much as it pains me to announce this. The school board felt that by ruining this time of year for Satan Claws in such a demeaning and underhanded manner that Kieron showed a creative ability in evil." Kazaik spat out the words, his eyes darkening as he spoke. "If I had my way, there wouldn't be creative evil in the world. However, since that is the official ruling, Kieron is free to return to school on Monday morning."

"What about Santa Claus. Are they going to reverse it?" Kieron's mother asked.

"Unfortunately not." Kazaik grimaced. "Due to extensive marketing opportunities and a good use of poverty, greed and sloth, they've decided it'll be a good way to introduce evil to people when they are young." He shook his head. "I disagree, but what do I know. I've only been a master of evil for seven thousand years," he muttered.

Kazaik scowled at Kieron, and his eyes glowed red. "What can I say, Lascher? I'll see you in class on Monday." His hands glowed red with anger as he turned on his heel and walked out of the room. "I'll let myself out."

Kieron stared at the back of his professor with his mouth hanging open.

Did I actually do something evil for once?

He watched the professor leave the house before turning to face his parents, who were still angry, judging by the murderous expressions on their faces.

"See, it's all okay." He smiled.

"Okay? You created the stupidest holiday in the universe!" His father shook a candy cane at him. "Do you know what these fucking things are even for?"

Kieron shook his head. "No, but this was all so I'd pass my exams, and I did, right? So the crisis is over, yes?"

His father crushed the candy cane up in his fist before shaking his head and muttering, 'I have an idiot for a son.' He stormed out of the room.

Kieron slumped into a nearby armchair, allowing a slow smile to spread across his face. He'd got through the exams, he'd saved the elves, he'd made this cold and miserable time of year into something beautiful and special for countless people and he'd got a new best friend. Overall, it had worked out really well for him.

"I don't know what you're smiling about. If you think this means you've learnt pure evil, you're delusional," his mother said.

He glanced up at her. "But the exam result says I've passed." He grinned.

She narrowed her eyes at him. "You've only passed the mock exam."

He frowned. He never did understand what the 'mock' part of the exam was. "What does that mean?"

"You still have to pass the real exam." She scowled at him.

"That wasn't the real exam?" he cried. "What the fuck was it then?"

"There's always a mock test before an exam." She shrugged.

"What the hell for?"

She grinned before silently leaving the room with a swish of her long emerald skirt.

Another exam? Now, that's just pure evil.

THE END

READ THE PREVIEW FOR

AN AWARD-WINNING NOVEL IN THE DEMON DIARIES

Demonic DORA

BEWITCHED IN HELL

CLAIRE CHILTON

1
HOLLOWED BE THY BRAIN

Dora Carridine rested her Doc Martens on the wooden church pew in front of her and idly cleaned her nails with a combat knife. She watched the small film crew set up around the podium at the front of the church while her father, the Reverend Theodore Carridine, had his hair fluffed into angelic white fuzz by a stylist.

She yawned. *Another bible bashing show coming soon to a TV near you!* She didn't ask for much in life, but she'd greatly appreciate it if the studio would cancel her father's embarrassing television show. She didn't pray to deities. Surely if there were such things as Gods, they'd have listened when she begged them to burn her mother alive for making her wear a cardigan in the eighth grade.

Dora had been a curious child, so when growing up in such a strict religious home, she'd tested out as many sins as she could. Lightning had never struck her down, she hadn't incurred the wrath of God and to be honest, if there was anyone up there watching, they didn't give a crap what she did.

"Now let us pray," her father said into the microphone when he stood at the podium, his face solemn.

Dora lowered her head and read the spell book in her lap. Images of demons and the blackest of magic filled the grimoire. She could barely read it. *I so wish I'd taken Latin now.*

"Our father, who art …" Her father recited. The large congregation chanted with him.

"… Who art embarrassing whenst he is on television," Dora mumbled out of habit. Two devout parishioners spun around and glowered at her. "Hollowed be thy brain," she added for their benefit and chuckled when they turned away from her in disgust.

It was going to be a long show today, and she was already bored – beyond death. She glanced around the large church. People around her were praying with their eyes closed. Even her producer mother had her eyes shut and wasn't watching the show. *Time to get outta here.*

Dora shoved her spell book down the waistband of her red miniskirt and carefully lowered her feet off the pew. She slid the knife into the scabbard inside her boot before silently sinking down in her seat. She slipped onto the hard stone floor, rolling on all fours before she crawled through the narrow space between the pews. She sped up when she left the benches behind and was out in the open, scurrying towards the confessional boxes.

She rested behind the dark mahogany box before peering back at the room. No one was watching her. They were all standing and preparing to sing a hymn. She stood up and walked into the alcove ahead, then climbed the stone staircase towards her room.

She brushed the dust off the knees of her red and black striped tights on her way up. *Lazy ass cleaners should be crucified for the mess they left the place in.*

When she reached the top of the stairs, she turned left at the large organ pipes, heading up the narrow stone passage of a second staircase which led to her attic room.

Dora's room was pretty cool. It was inside the spire of the old church, offering her privacy from the rest of the world. She pushed open the ancient oak door. It made a loud, ominous creak – just how she liked it. The room was not decorated to her liking with baby pink walls and a matching carpet. The little princess room was her parents' doing. She couldn't count the number of times she'd spray painted blood-red pentagrams or black demon art on the walls of this room. Every time she came back from school, it was back to princess pink with decorative voile hanging over the bed and pink fluffy throw cushions on the furniture.

Bile rose in her throat when she glanced down at the pink floral-print duvet. She swallowed and knelt on the floor at the end of her bed before pulling out the large white plastic sheet from beneath it. The sheet was actually the back of a Twister mat, but it worked just as well for a dark arts summoning circle. She had painted a black and red pentagram on it to put it to a darker use than it was intended for, meaning she had to ensure it was well hidden from her parents at all times.

She shivered with excitement. Today was going to be her day. After years of trying and failing, she was finally going to cast a spell that would work. Despite years of failure, her inability to summon a demon hadn't dimmed her enthusiasm. The Wicca group at the local magical supply store would be laughing at her on the other side of their white-light Earth-mother faces if she pulled this off.

Dora was going to summon a demon, and not just a normal demon. No, she was going for a high-level demon that would be under her control. *The first thing he's going to do for me is make this room red.*

She placed six black candles around her makeshift summoning circle and lit them one by one. She put an ornate pottery bowl at the center of the circle and threw a mixture of herbs into it. Next, she pulled the knife out of her boot and made a small cut on her thumb with it. She watched her blood slowly drip into the bowl until there were six drops. Then she pressed her thumb against her leg. Once the cut had stopped bleeding, she dropped the knife and dragged her schoolbag over to her. She reached inside it, feeling for the small box in the bottom of the bag.

The secret ingredient was a Karabashi bloodstone. She carefully opened the small black box and stared at the red shiny stone in awe. It looked like a glass ball filled with blood. She'd searched high and low for one when she'd found the spell in her book. None of the usual haunts had one; not the antiques shop or even the specialist magic supply store. She had tried everywhere and had nearly given up altogether. One stormy night when she'd been staring at the dark skies, she'd had a moment of clarity. After some tough negotiation, she'd got it on Ebay.

Dora put the bloodstone in the bowl and picked up the grimoire. Her heart thundered in her chest. It was going to work, it was – she could feel it. She carefully read the spell and closed her eyes, chanting with a faith she'd never felt before. Six times she repeated the spell, and she waited.

She held her breath. A demon was going to appear – he was! Her clock ticked loudly as she sat cross-legged in front of her summoning circle, waiting. After a few silent moments, she let out her breath in an exhausted sigh. *Nothing again. Nothing ever works!*

She abruptly stood up and kicked over the bowl, shattering the bloodstone inside it. The thick, gloopy liquid slithered across the broken glass and mingled inside the bowl. She didn't bother to glance at it. She stormed out of her room and slammed the door shut behind her. *Nothing ever bloody works!*

Once Dora had left the room, a fire ignited in the center of the circle, and the Twister mat curled up as it became inflamed in the fires of hell.

2

HELL ON EARTH

J osie Carridine watched from the front row pew as sweat dripped down her husband's face while he shouted at the TV cameras from the pulpit, threatening the wrath of God to all sinners. She nodded in agreement when he declared all vegetarians were an abomination. She was surely blessed to have such a righteous man for a husband. Not only had he saved her from a life of sin, pole dancing at the infamous 'Big Fat Joint', he'd also helped her career as a TV producer. Oh yes, life was wonderful once you left sin behind.

"And He shall strike you down," Theodore shouted out to his congregation. "Down to the depths of hell if – I-if …"

Theodore stopped speaking and stared at the back of the church with his mouth hanging open and his eyes widening. Josie jumped when she heard a loud scream from the back of the room. She spun around to look behind her while hearing the entire congregation shifting in their seats as they did the same.

Thick black swirls of smoke were twirling in the air around the closed doors of the church. *Has someone set the doors on fire?* She gaped at the fog in shock and shook her head at the thought. The mist wasn't behaving like smoke at all. It amassed into a big black blob with more and more seeping in under the door until it split into two foggy shadows.

She lifted her glasses, which were hanging around her neck, to peer through them. The two black smoky shapes formed into separate entities that appeared to have heads and arms. She dropped her glasses and rubbed her eyes before looking again.

At the same time, both shadows snapped open fiery red eyes. Their maws gaped as they let out a loud hollow laugh that echoed through the church.

Josie winced when Mrs Smiggins, the oldest member of the congregation, keeled over three aisles down. *I hope she's fainted, and she's not dead.*

The two shadows each gripped a handle of the double doors of the church and flung them open. A burst of flames shot through the entrance. Gale force winds blasted through the room, knocking parishioners over and sending the smaller ones flying around the church in a twister style hurricane.

Josie ducked down in her seat and hugged the pew, which was thankfully nailed down.

"Out, damned demon." She heard Theodore shout at the shadows, but they had already evaporated into the flames. Lightning shot around the high ceiling of the church, shattering through the stained-glass windows. The air was alive with electricity.

Josie fell to her knees and prayed – and this time she meant it. *Dear God, please save me from this nightmare. I promise to be faithful and end my affair with Phil on camera four. I'll remain good and pious, and stop trying to sell ad space on the church website. Amen.*

She glanced up to see an army of turquoise

serpents slithering through the doors and up the aisles towards the congregation, who were now screaming and running towards the pulpit to escape the demon snakes. She pulled herself up and jumped back as one of the snakes snapped at her hand, almost succeeding in ripping one of her fingers off. She pulled away just in time. They were like no snakes she'd ever seen before. Their eyes were ocean-blue, and their teeth were green. *Have they been drinking NiQuil?*

The snake reared up. It was as tall as she was. Fear slammed through her, making her knees tremble. It launched at her, emitting a deadly hiss. She threw her bible at it, knocking it backwards before she dashed towards the podium and cowered behind her husband, who continued to pray, although his voice was now hoarse.

The wind howled around them. The parishioners who hadn't passed out were all cowering around the pulpit. Some were white with shock, others were openly crying with thick trails of snot pouring out of their noses. They were the lucky ones, to have stuffed up noses. A few of the congregation had crapped their pants, judging by the stains on their clothes and the stench in the air.

Josie stared towards the blazing fires at the entrance as they wickedly licked the inside of the church. She glanced down the aisle in horror as her gaze fell upon the blue snakes writhing around at the foot of the raised pulpit, hissing and biting at each other. There was no way out.

She jumped when deep thunder echoed through the room and glanced up to see violent winds rip apart the inside of the chapel. Streaks of lighting shot around the small group of people huddled on the pulpit, making them scream and jerk in terror. Wailing pleas for God to help could be heard over the howling wind while the hurricane twisted its way up the church, about to engulf them.

Josie gasped at several loud stomps. The church shook violently before everything disappeared. The snakes vanished, the wind died down, the lightning stopped and the fire faded into nothing.

"Shit!" Dora cried as she walked back into her room and saw her carpet burning. She repeatedly stamped

on the fire until the last ember turned to black ash.

"Crap," she said. *Dad's going to go ballistic over this.*

Dora sighed at the useless summoning circle, which was now a curled up, burnt mess. She threw herself onto her bed and lay on her stomach, staring at the black screen of her pink television. She pulled the remote control from beneath the mattress and pressed the power button on it. Her TV was only allowed one network – her father's. She wasn't allowed to watch anything else. Thank Beelzebub her parents weren't net savvy, or she would be living in a religious bubble.

Since it was her bedtime, she knew the stupid show would be over soon. Sometimes the old black and white movies they showed late at night weren't too bad. Doris Day kicked ass in Calamity Jane.

The television flickered into life, and her dad's show appeared on the screen. People were wailing, crying, and praising the Lord. *Aww shit, they didn't do another one of those miracle cures shows, did they?*

Dora's eyes widened as Molly Carmichael, the

prim librarian from the main library, wandered in front of the camera mumbling incoherently. Molly turned her back to the camera and bowed to the pulpit. Dora's eyes widened more when she saw what she could only describe as effervescent shit stains decorating the back of Molly's pink tweed skirt. She watched Molly wander off camera, still mumbling random words like, 'snakes' and 'demons' as she disappeared from view.

For the first time ever, Dora found herself glued to her dad's show. *I can't believe I missed this.*

Her father finally came on screen as he pulled himself up off the floor. He clawed at the podium and dragged himself up, so his head appeared over it. He was shaking all over and had a few small cuts and gashes on his face. His hair looked like an oversized white afro hovering around his head. The priest's collar of his vestments hung limply down his neck in a white line.

"Dah ..." He tried to speak, but his voice was so hoarse he only managed a sound. He was breathing hard. Judging by the murderous look in his eyes, Dora knew whatever he was about to say was not going to be good.

"Dohh ..." He managed before taking a deep breath. He stared down at the podium for a moment in silent fury.

He eventually looked straight up into the camera. The moans and wails of parishioners were echoing behind him, through the microphone. "D-Do-Dora, I'm going to kill you!" Her father gasped into the camera before he passed out on the podium and slid to the floor.

Dora blinked at the screen. *Shit, what am I getting blamed for now?*

K ieron Lascher stopped chasing turquoise snakes when a burst of light exploded in the darkness a few feet away from him. He frowned and walked over to it. It was a hole ripped through the ether, a jagged tear of light in his dark and dismal world.

He reached out his hand and touched the shimmering light. It was warm and sticky. He pulled his hand back and glanced around him. There was no one around. Even the twittering hell spawn were up to no good elsewhere today. It wasn't surprising since it was only a couple of weeks until Judgment Day. Everyone was cramming for the finals.

Kieron knew he should be studying too. His father would eviscerate him if he failed this time. He had been revising all morning, trying to catch a snake for an experiment, but he had just ended up with several bites off the bloody things.

He tried not to let it bother him, but he was a failure at being evil. Nothing ever worked out. He got the formulas right, but it just never turned out evil enough. If he failed his test this year, he would be expelled from Hell. Everyone knew what that meant. A fate worse than colonic irrigation – he would be exiled to Earth.

Kieron had never been to Earth. He'd been born in Hell, but he'd seen it through the various portals. He shuddered at the thought of it. He'd seen the monotonous work humans had to do; filing, spread sheets … homework! Humans were sorry creatures; they followed dreams of things they'd never have, and they were powerless in the world they lived in. He couldn't imagine anything worse. No, he had to pass the test this year – being exiled to Earth was not an option.

He tilted his head while he studied the tear of

light. After a few minutes of contemplation, he decided the best plan was to fix it. It was dangerous leaving a gaping hole in the ether lying around like this. Someone might fall into it and hurt themselves.

He ran his fingers over the edges and encountered the warm sticky feeling again. *What kind of tear is it?* It pulsed as if it were alive. He'd never seen a portal like it, but there were a lot of lunatic demons practicing spells at this time of year. It was obviously a mistake because no talented warlock would create something so messy.

The wind howled around him in harsh, warm gusts. He glanced back and stared at the desolate horizon. *Are the volcanoes playing up again?* A vice-like grip clamped onto his wrist, which was still hovering over the tear in reality. He yelped when it tugged on his arm. The tear growled as it became a vortex, sucking things into it with howling winds and a terrifying force. Snakes and shrubbery shot past him as the growing hole consumed them. The ground shifted towards the portal, and the red sands of the barren landscape swirled around him. He attempted to scream but could only cough as the sand blew into his mouth.

He pulled back against the vacuum, trying to free himself from the portal, but the force was too powerful. He finally managed to cry out for help, but the sound was lost in the din. Using every muscle in his body, he tried to detach from the pulsing gash in reality. The power of the suction increased, lifting him off the ground before the portal pulled him into another realm.

Kieron squeezed his eyes shut as a blinding light flashed around him. His stomach leapt into his throat. The force of the pull flattened his cheeks to his skull. Every nerve in his body screamed in protest as gravity crushed it. He warily opened one eye, just in time to see the tear become a distant shadow. Flashes of bright lights sped past him. He crashed into something soft and expelled a shocked yelp of pain. Everything went dark as the portal closed.

He fought to suppress the urge to throw up while using his hands to search around in the dark. He could feel cloth draping over him and sharp painful blocks underneath him. He blindly explored his surroundings with his hands. The space was confined. He could feel the walls around him by simply stretching out his arms. He tried to control a bubble of panic when the thought of all those snakes being in here with him filled his mind.

His hand hit something on a string, a pendulum of some kind. He felt around for it in the darkness. It was wildly swinging around, but he caught it in his grasp on the third try. The heavy, metal object was hanging from twine. He tugged it to see if it would hold his weight. A bright light burst into the small room, and he found himself looking up the inside of a girl's dress. It would have been a pleasant experience had there been a girl inside the dress, but alas the dress was empty.

Something sharp dug into his backside, so he rooted around with his hands to pull the object out from beneath him. He stared at the shiny ruby slipper in his hand. The three-inch heel and pointed toe on the shoe answered some questions for him. *I'm in a witch's closet!*

Kieron pushed the clothes out of the way and got to his feet, ripping half of the dresses off their hangers in the process. He surveyed the inside of the closet before turning to face the slatted door. He inhaled a sharp breath when he stared through the gaps in the door and saw the witch.

She lay on a pink bed at the center of the room with her ebony hair twisted up in knots. Her blood-red lips pouted seductively at something she was watching. She was appealing to look at. Her long legs idly swung in the air behind her. She wore a pair of tiny red shorts and some kind of white tunic that had no sleeves. She was the first witch Kieron had ever seen, but his father had told him about them. They were all sexy little minxes with nasty tricks up their sleeves. He remembered seduction was their greatest trick, but he wasn't worried. He was pretty smooth with the ladies. He'd had the best tutors – succubae.

Kieron became aware of his own body swaying while he watched her legs swing back and forth behind her. *Hypnosis!* He realized and quickly averted his eyes up to the top of the closet, trying to calm his racing pulse. He refused to look at the witch and stared upwards. Piled on the shelf at the top of the closet were boxes and boxes of mysterious witch items. He tilted his head, trying to read the labels before reaching up to pull down the top box on the pile. It was red and white, the colors of blood and life. *It must be one of her darkest secrets.* It was labeled with one thick black word. He tried to pronounce the word in his mind. *Mono-Polly.* He didn't know this language, but it must be immensely powerful to have such colors on it. He took a deep breath and opened the box while his heart hammered.

Inside was an odd-looking ritual board. *What kind of casting can you do with this?* It had places on it with haunting names like 'Marylebone Station' and 'The Strand'. There were strange tarot cards called 'Chance' and 'Community Chest'. He recognized small silver ritual symbols of pagan items like the iron and the boot, but they were mixed in with symbols he hadn't seen before. He gasped when he picked up the small icon of a dog, dropping the box in shock. *What kind of monster is this witch? She'd cast upon a helpless hound.*

He nearly screamed when he looked through the slats in the door and saw her staring straight at him. She sat up on the bed and began making her way over to the closet. He inwardly cursed himself for making such a racket when he dropped the box.

He found his eyes drawn to her ample bosom when she stood up. *Think clean thoughts, think clean thoughts,* he told himself. *This minx will not turn me into her demon slave, no matter how bouncy they look. Er, she looks.*

He froze, overcome with a feeling of helplessness when she walked towards the door, reaching for the handle.

Her chamber door burst open, and a deranged holy man with wild white hair stormed into the room. He carried a crucifix in one hand and a bag of salt in the other. Kieron involuntarily hissed as the witch spun around to face the man, instinctively glancing down as his eyes were drawn to her ass.

"BACK DEMON!" Dora forgot about the noise in her closet as she spun around to face her father. He held a crucifix in front of him and appeared slightly crazed. His vestments were ripped and dirty, his hair was sticking out in a wild afro, and the insane gleam in his eyes could only mean one thing — exorcism time.

Dora backed away from him to the center of the room. "Dad, come on. Whatever I did, I didn't mean it," she said, holding her hands up in an attempt to placate him.

"SILENCE DEMON!" He bellowed before waving his cross at her.

"Oh, for fuc – ahhh …" Dora yawned in mid-argument. *Screw it, I can't be bothered. Just entertain his insanity, and you'll get to bed faster.*

She obediently stood in the center of the room while watching her father pour a circle of salt onto the floor around her. He shouted scripture at her, causing her to yawn again. Through bleary eyes, she studied him as he rushed to the wall and began nailing crosses to it around the doorframe. Sweat poured down his red face while he hammered the last cross into the wall.

He turned towards her, his knuckles turning white as he tightly gripped the bag of salt. "This will hold you, demon. Tomorrow you shall be sent back to Hell."

"Okay, Dad." Dora rubbed her eyes with her fists, hoping he would bugger off soon, so she could go back to bed.

Her father lined the window ledge with salt, then the doorway before carefully stepping over it and leaving the room. "You'll burn for your sins." He told her before he closed the door.

"Okie dokie." She agreed as the door slammed shut. She shook her head at the insanity of her life.

Just before she stepped out of the circle, the door to her closet burst open. An attractive blond-haired boy with bright blue eyes fell through the door. He wore a swashbuckler's shirt and tight leather pants. "Don't worry, Minx-witch. I shall save you!" he cried.

Dora gasped and swung her fist out at the strange boy. Her fist made a solid connection with his jaw and sent him flipping over face first onto the floor. She looked down at his unconscious body and sighed. "Okay, if you must." She had a feeling it was going to be a long night.

4

Witches & Bitches

Dora studied the unconscious guy sprawled face down on her puce carpet. He was gorgeous even with his mouth hanging open and a bit of drool coming out of it. He had high cheekbones, a strong jawline, smooth tanned skin, broad shoulders and a perfect ass. She inclined her head sideways and checked out his backside. He was wearing a pair of tight brown leather pants. It was almost hypnotic watching his buttocks randomly flex.

She opened the leather pouch she had stolen from his belt. It was the closest thing he had to a wallet. It didn't contain money or any kind of identification, only a range of colorful gems. Given his choice of clothing and the contents of his pouch, she could only assume he was a crazy pirate. *That makes no sense. What would a pirate be doing in*

Berkville?

The boy groaned, and she sighed with relief. She was glad she hadn't done any serious damage to him. He rolled over onto his back and gazed up at her with sleepy eyes. Little bursts of electricity tingled all over her body when his bright blue eyes scanned her from head to toe in lazy appreciation.

He smiled as he stretched his arms across the carpet, arching his back in the process. He paused when his fingers trailed over the circle of salt beside him. He briefly glanced at the salt and then back to Dora. His eyes widened in an instant, and his smile slipped. He jumped up yelping and frantically searching the room for something. "Oww! It burns, it burns," he cried, shaking his hand as if trying to get the grains of salt off it.

"What does?" She ran to his side to try and help, but he pushed her away during his desperate search of her room.

"Wash it off, the salt. Please, wash it off." He begged as he wildly waved his hand around.

Dora snatched his hand out of the air, tightly gripping his wrist while she examined it. His palm was large and masculine compared to her small hands. The skin was smooth and tanned like the rest of him, but there wasn't a mark on it. It certainly wasn't burning. "It's not burning," she said as she showed him it.

He stopped dancing around like a lunatic and glanced down, peering at his hand in awe. Confusion furrowed his brow as she brushed the grains of salt off his palm.

"It's supposed to be burning." He peered up, and their eyes locked.

Her skin heated up, and a shiver trembled up her back. "Umm, why?" She attempted to appear unaffected by his close proximity.

"Because it's salt," he said, implying she should know what he meant.

Dora didn't know what to make of him. She just stared at him.

"Minx-witch, you should know these things." He told her.

"Who?" she asked. Why did he keep calling her that? His warm fingers massaged her hand before they traveled up to her wrist and arm.

"Okay, enough games," he said with defeat in his tone, but his eyes were sparkling with something else. "You win."

"Wha –" She didn't finish as he pulled her into his arms and kissed her. His hard body pressed against her, and his warm hands roamed up her back. She almost melted into his wicked kisses – almost.

Dora pushed him away. "What the hell do you

think you're doing?"

"Becoming your willing slave." He winked at her and rested his hands on her hips.

Her heart did a little backflip. "Fine. Clean my room," she replied. *Heart, behave yourself. Who the hell is this guy?*

"Uh, I'm not that kind of slave. That's not my purpose."

"Your purpose? What the hell were you doing in my closet? Who are you?" She stepped back and untangled herself from his embrace in case he attacked her again. She could handle many things; violence, robbery even religious zealots, but someone being nice to her and kissing her was a whole new experience.

"Oh, how rude of me." He dipped his head in a short bow before raising her hand to his lips and kissing it. "Let me introduce myself. I am Lord Kieron D. Lascher."

Dora snatched her hand back before he kissed anything else and caused her brain to shrink. "What does the 'D' stand for?"

"Oh, er, Derek," he mumbled. "And you are?"

"Derek?" She expelled a surprised giggle.

"It means ruler." He appeared offended. "What's your name, Minx-witch?" he snapped.

"Dora Carridine."

"Hmm, and *you* mock my name?" Kieron pouted at her.

"Sorry," she mumbled, laughing. "It was fun – wait. Who the hell are you and what were you doing in my closet? Did Dad put you in there?"

"Does your father often put young men in your closet late at night?" Kieron asked. He appeared genuinely curious.

"Er, not so far, but you never know with him."

"I cannot confirm who put me in your closet, for I do not know. But I was ripped from my home and brought here for a reason. The longer I am here, the more I realize that it was the fates that sent me." He studied her for a moment. "I believe I have been sent here for you. In fact, I am sure of it."

The words made something inside Dora heat up, and a shiver trembled through her body. Maybe it was because he looked so honorable and hot when he said it. Also, what girl wouldn't love a guy that fate sent to her?

"What makes you think that?" she asked.

"You clearly need saving. It is simply a question of from what?" He slowly walked around her. "You are a minx-witch who is trapped in a tower by an evil holy man. Perhaps I am to save you from him?"

He'd been standing behind her for a while. She wondered what he was doing back there, so she spun

around and caught him staring at the place her ass had been a few moments earlier. She scowled at him.

"Clearly you are also lacking in your skills as a minx if your kisses are anything to go by. Perhaps my duty is to teach you seduction." He grinned as he leapt at her, knocking her onto the bed and pinning her down by the wrists. "Would you like that?"

Dora acted on instinct. She kneed him in the balls as hard as she could before pushing him off her.

He rolled sideways onto the bed and curled up in agony. "Why would you do that?" he cried. "What kind of demon-witch are you?"

"One who is perfectly capable of taking care of herself," she replied as she got off the bed and picked up a heavy vase. "Try that again, and I'll knock you senseless – again!"

He held up his hands in submission and sat up on the bed. "So, why am I here? Why else would I be here if not to help you?" He appeared to be genuinely confused.

"Where did you come from?" she asked. She needed to know who this guy was. All she knew so far was he used old-fashioned words, and he was a bit of a perv.

"Hell," he said, waving his hand in the air as if to brush the question away. "Sinner's Hall, the fifth level."

Dora stared at him in awe. "Hell? Y-y-you're a demon?"

"Obviously," he said, appearing a bit upset that she hadn't already known that. "Can't you tell by my evil ways?"

"Well, er, no." She studied his handsome face and attractive body. "Aren't demons supposed to have horns?"

"Only hell spawn have them on the outside. The main demons are just –"

"Horny?" She cut in.

Kieron flashed a wicked grin.

Dora shook her head. "I can't believe I ask for a demon lord, and I get *you*."

"Hey! I am a demon lord." He shot her an annoyed glance. "A big evil one, a master of destruction ..."

She peered in her closet. "Dress destruction?"

"That wasn't my fault."

"Uh huh, how exactly are *you* evil? You came here to save me!"

"And to defile you, of course." He defended his evil ways.

"Okay, so ... I summoned you. That makes you my bitch, right?"

"I do not know that term." He sounded confused.

"Bitch? It means slave or servant, but in a good and manly way." Dora grinned.

"Ah, I see. Yes Minx-witch-Dora, I am your bitch."

She stifled a giggle. "Right then, *My Bitch*, there will be no defiling of me, and you will do as I command, understand?"

"Not even a little bit of defiling?" A disappointed expression appeared on his face.

"No, none at all."

"Evildoing?" His blue eyes shone with hope.

"There probably will be some evildoing." She admitted.

"Okay, that sounds good." Kieron agreed.

"Good. Now, I'm tired. It's been a really long day, so I'm going to go to bed, and I suggest you do the same." She told him before she climbed into bed and hugged her pillow.

The bed trembled as he got off it, and she snuggled under her blanket. The bed bounced as a weight landed on it. A hot body pressed against her back, and a strong masculine arm snaked around her waist.

"Bitch."

"Yes, my minx." His hot breath warmed the back of her neck.

"What are you doing?"

"Sleeping."

"Not in my bed."

"Oh come on! What's a shared bed between a master and their minion?"

Dora rolled over and pushed him off the bed with as much force as she could muster.

"Fine." He snapped, pushing himself off the floor. "I'll sleep in the closet."

"Good bitch," she said, stifling a laugh as he stomped over to the closet, walked into it and slammed the door shut behind him.

After a few minutes, she began to worry about Kieron. *There isn't enough room in the closet for him to lie down.* With a sigh, she climbed out of bed and walked over to the closet door, deciding he'd be fine with a sleeping bag on the floor, instead.

Dora opened the door while trying to think of the best way to suggest he should sleep on her floor. She blinked at the scene inside her closet. Kieron lay on a round king-sized waterbed adorned with red silk sheets and an array of opulent pillows and blankets. The closet had been transformed into a large room with everything from a minibar to a couch fitting comfortably inside it.

He glanced up at her with a devilish grin. "I knew you'd change your mind, my frisky little minx. There's room for two." He winked.

"Bitch," she said before slamming the door on him. She walked away from the closet and climbed back into her pink bed, hugging her blanket and trying not to think about devilish demons.

Sleep, she told herself. *Maybe when I wake up the world will be sane again.*

READ MORE

Buy the book online at:

WWW.CLAIRE−CHILTON.COM

A MUST-READ NOVEL IN THE DEMON DIARIES

Deceased
DORA

DORA CARRIDINE
BEWITCHED
IN DEATH

CLAIRE CHILTON

After being expelled from Hell, she woke up in her own coffin...

When Dora Carridine wakes up in her coffin, the first thing she plans to do is find out what happened to her friends since they were also exiled from Hell. But Dora didn't come back entirely human, and everyone keeps trying to kill her.

If she manages to avoid being bitten by an over-amorous, Victorian vampire, being captured by the Vatican and being roasted alive by her neighbors, then hopefully she can find Kieron and find out what she really is.

But first, she has to put an end to an ancient war amongst the paranormal beings on Earth. How hard can that be, right?

OUT NOW

WWW.CLAIRE-CHILTON.COM

CONTINUE READING WITH

A BESTSELLING NOVEL IN THE DEMON DIARIES

Divine
DORA
BEWITCHED IN HEAVEN

CLAIRE CHILTON

Heaven just turned out to be worse than Hell!

After being killed, Dora Carridine was shipped off to
Heaven, but she's not ready to give up her life just yet,
especially not when it means spending eternity in Angel boot
camp.

She does everything in her power to try to get home, but
nothing works. Even if she manages to escape Camp Angel
and survive the sadistic drill sergeant, she still doesn't know
how to get her body back.

Powerless and alone, she decides that there is only one thing
she can do. Dora has to find God, and hope he's not a
sanctimonious dick.

WWW.CLAIRE-CHILTON.COM

CAN'T WAIT FOR CLAIRE CHILTON'S NEXT STORY?

Let her know by leaving stars and telling her what

you liked about

A HINT OF HELL

in a review!

FREE BOOKS

Enjoy Claire Chilton's free books. Try out her

other series for free or read more of this series on

any device with **Free Reads**.

claire-chilton.com/free-books

WANT TO TALK TO OTHER FANS?

Visit *claire-chilton.com* and join the discussion.

AUTHOR

After completing her honors degree in English Literature, Claire Chilton was interviewed to work for MI5. Fortunately, for the sake of the United Kingdom, she did not get the job. Now a web designer and graphic designer with a passion for great stories, she writes about the adventures she'd like to have.

A prolific writer with wide-ranging interests, Claire specializes in romantic and speculative fiction, which includes genres such as mystery, science fiction, fantasy, horror, comedy and romance. Her mystery romance novel, *Hustle*, won Harlequin's *So You Think You Can Write* contest in 2013, and her previous books in *The Demon Diaries* won the *Most Read* award on Wattpad.

After exploring the world in her misspent youth, traveling across Europe, Africa, and the Caribbean, she now lives in an ancient Roman city in Yorkshire with her Californian husband and a fluffy kitten called Shadow, who is convinced she is a bigger cat than she is.

You can find Claire online at **claire-chilton.com**.